Pirate Pat

Turn the page to start the story.

The night was cold,
the sky was black,
the window rattled...

Pirate Pat

Written by Mairi Mackinnon

Illustrated by Mike and Carl Gordon

How this book works

The story of **Pirate Pat** has been written for you to read with your child. You take turns to read:

You read these words.

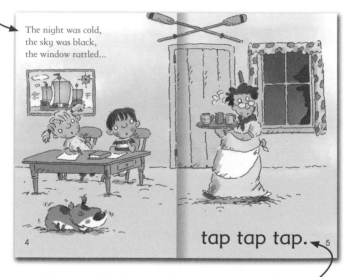

The night was cold,
the sky was black,
the window rattled...

tap tap tap.

Your child reads these words.

You don't have to finish the story in one session. If your child is getting tired, put a marker in the page and come back to it later.

You can find out more about helping your child with this book, and with reading in general, on pages 30-31.

tap tap tap.

"There's someone there,
I'm sure of it!
Sam, do stop barking."

Sit Sam sit.

Well, we were scared,
but not our Gran.
She went to look:

it is a man.

A tattered coat,
a huge black hat...
Look – it's a pirate!

Pat hunted in
his heavy pack.
What has he found?

It is a map.

"But that's my home!"
says Gran. "Look, lad,
you can't just dig here."

Pat is sad.

He starts to frown.
Ooh, this looks bad!
Gran says, "I mean it!"

Pat is mad.

But does he listen?
Not a bit!
Now look at him –

Pat in a pit.

A bang, a clang,
what has he hit?
A treasure chest!
Pat shouts,

21

22

Puzzle 1

Look at the pictures together
and try retelling the story.

1.

2.

3.

4.

5.

6.

Why don't you talk about what they might all do next?

Puzzle 2

Choose the right word for each picture.

1.

Sam	sad

2.

man	map

3.

pan

Pat

4.

pit

sit

Puzzle 3

Find the words that rhyme. The first pair has already been linked as an example.

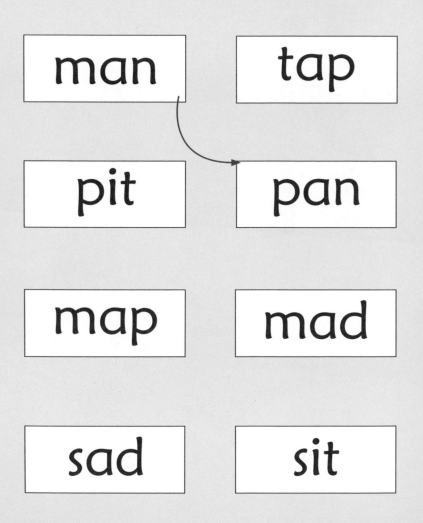

Answers to puzzles

Puzzle 1

Use this puzzle to check that your child has understood the story, and have fun discussing what might happen next.

If your child isn't sure what to say, try asking leading questions such as, "Who's this? What are they doing now?" (Of course, there is more than one possible answer.)

Puzzle 2

1. Sam   2. map
3. Pat   4. pit

Puzzle 3

man ⁓ pan
pit ⁓ sit
map ⁓ tap
sad ⁓ mad

Guidance notes

Usborne Very First Reading is a series of books, specially developed for children who are learning to read. In the early books in the series, you and your child take turns to read, and your child steadily builds the knowledge and confidence to read alone.

The words for your child to read in **Pirate Pat** use only these eight letters:

These are often the first letters that children learn to read at school. With just eight letters, your child can already start reading simple words and sentences. Later books in the series gradually introduce more letters, sounds and spelling patterns, while reinforcing the ones your child already knows.

You'll find lots more information about the structure of the series, advice on helping your child with reading, extra practice activities and games on the Very First Reading website,* **www.usborne.com/veryfirstreading**

*US readers go to **www.veryfirstreading.com**

Some questions and answers

- **Why do I need to read with my child?**
  Sharing stories and taking turns makes reading an enjoyable and fun activity for children. It also helps them to develop confidence and reading stamina, and to take part in an exciting story using very few words.

- **When is a good time to read?**
  Choose a time when you are both relaxed, but not too tired, and there are no distractions. Only read for as long as your child wants to – you can always try again another day.

- **What if my child gets stuck?**
  Don't simply read the problem word yourself, but prompt your child and try to find the right answer together. Similarly, if your child makes a mistake, go back and look at the word together. Don't forget to give plenty of praise and encouragement.

- **We've finished, now what do we do?**
  It's a good idea to read the story several times to give your child more practice and confidence. Then you can try reading **Double Trouble** at the same level or, when your child is ready, go on to Book 2 in the series.

Edited by Jenny Tyler and Lesley Sims
Designed by Russell Punter

First published in 2010 by Usborne Publishing Ltd., Usborne House,
83-85 Saffron Hill, London EC1N 8RT, England. www.usborne.com
Copyright © 2010 Usborne Publishing Ltd.